ASHES TO NEW

an Angel Fire Rock Romance Prequel

ELLIE MASTERS

Ashes to New:

an Angel Fire Rock Romance Prequel

Copyright © 2016 by Ellie Masters

All rights reserved.

Image/art disclaimer: Licensed material is being used for illustrative purposes only. Any person depicted in the licensed material is a model.

Editor: Jovana Shirley, Unforeseen Editing, www.unforeseenediting.com

Cover Artist: Ellie Masters

Images: stock.adobe.com

Interior Design/Formatting: Ellie Masters

Published in the United States of America

JEM Publishing, LLC

This is a work of fiction. While reference might be made to actual historical events or existing locations, the names, characters, businesses, places, and incidents are either the product of the author's imagination or are used fictitiously, and any resemblance to actual persons, living or dead, business establishments, events, or locales is entirely coincidental.

* * * *

ISBN: 0997845023
ISBN13: 978-0-9978450-2-0

Ellie Masters

Ashes to New

* * * *

Warning

This book contains sexually explicit scenes and adult language and might be considered offensive to some readers. This book is for sale to adults ONLY, as defined by the laws of the country where you made your purchase. Please store your books wisely and where they cannot be accessed by underage readers. This story is a story of surviving abuse. As such, it may present triggers to some individuals. I have taken care to protect the reader as much as possible, but triggers may still be present for some. Heed this warning, and enter with your eyes and heart open.

* * * *

Dedication

This book is dedicated to my one and only, my amazing and wonderful husband. Without your care and support, my writing would not have made it this far. You make me whole every day. I love you that much, which means from the beginning to the end and every point in between. Thank you, my dearest love, my heart and soul, for putting up with me, for believing in me, and for loving me as I brought these characters from my mind to the page.

* * * *

Acknowledgments

This book wouldn't have been possible without the tireless work of my critique team. I couldn't have done this without their help. I would like to thank my critique group at CritiqueCircle.com who ripped and shredded and helped me to make Ashes to New: an Angel Fire Rock Romance novella *something I can be proud to introduce to the world. I have learned and continue to learn with every word, every phrase, sentence, and chapter from my critique group.*

I'd also like to thank my PA, Sophie Lynn for her tireless guidance through the world of social media, late night calls, and endless support through the ups as well as the downs. This wouldn't be as much fun without you. My dear friend and Street Team

Manager, Nathalie Pinette, is my lifeline. She is a true saint, who saved me more times than I'm willing to admit. NAT has cheered with me, for me, and held my hand too many times, a tireless supporter, I adore her.

To my Beta readers, Shea Moran, Jennifer Hanna Guffey, and Phoenix Rose, thank you for taking a peek at this and smoothing off the last rough edges before Ashes to New hit the world. It means the world to me to have you be a part of my team.

I'd also like to thank my editor, Jovana Shirley. She graciously accepted a tight deadline and worked tirelessly to dress up my baby for its first tentative steps into the world. There aren't enough words. Thank you!

* * * *

To My Readers

This book is a work of fiction. It does not exist in the real world and should not be construed as reality. As in most fiction, I've taken liberties. I'd like to dedicate this book to all survivors of abuse. Your story is uniquely yours, and your path through it is one only you have walked. I applaud your strength and pray you find you way to a brighter day.

Love,
Ellie

CHAPTER ONE

WITH A HEAVY sigh, Elsbeth followed her fellow students into the embrace of summer. To them, it represented freedom, but for Elsbeth, the endless days would be nothing but a stretch of time to endure.

The halls of Carl Sandburg High School were filled with the shouts and raucous cheers of her classmates. A generalized mayhem celebrated the end of another year of school. Students emptied lockers of books, folders, and laptops. Old spiral-bound notebooks, along with mounds of papers no one cared about anymore, filled trash cans lining the halls.

While Elsbeth's classmates rushed to say their good-byes, she walked in a cocoon of silence, gripping the contents of her locker tight to her chest, as she kept her gaze set three feet forward, avoiding any and all eye contact with her peers.

But she couldn't avoid all attention.

Mr. Peterson leaned against the doorframe leading into his chemistry lab. He was talking with Scott Masterson, a junior, like Elsbeth. Scott was wildly popular, a jock with a brain, who got straight A's and was working toward a football scholarship, the ticket to his future. She envied him for his freedom to pursue his goals.

"You'd better behave this summer." Mr. Peterson's voice was stern but caring. "We need our star player to make it to State next year."

Yes, sir," Scott said, combing his fingers through the mop

.ngs covering his forehead. He noticed her then. "Hey, Elz," he

.lled out. "Got plans for tonight? A bunch of us are going to the movies. You want to come?"

Scott had been trying to get her to go on a date for the better half of the last semester. She'd always been too busy—not a complete lie, but other things filled her evenings and weekends. It simply wasn't cheering or band or volleyball team or dating.

With a shake of her head, she declined...again. "Sorry, but I've got plans, and my foster father isn't keen on the whole dating scene."

"Ah, it doesn't have to be a date. It's just a bunch of us hanging out."

Hugging her books, she stamped down the wave of anxiety building in her chest. "I'm sorry. I'd love to, but..." But she simply couldn't.

The hopefulness of his expression fell. "Maybe another time?"

She gave a fractional nod. "Sounds good."

Moving to the center of the crowded hall, she made a move to escape the awkward exchange, but Mr. Peterson stopped her in her tracks.

"Elsbeth." His words hit her in the chest and stopped the trudge of her feet.

"Yes, Mr. Peterson?"

The softness of his gaze tunneled straight to her heart, destabilizing her shields.

"You weren't going to leave without saying good-bye to your favorite chemistry teacher, were you?" Mr. Peterson spread his arms out wide, welcoming her into his personal space.

Elsbeth curled her lower lip inward, biting hard. While she adored Mr. Peterson and he was, without a doubt, her favorite teacher, to be that close to a man had her insides churning. But, with his arms outstretched, she couldn't refuse, not without raising eyebrows—or worse.

"Be safe this summer." He folded her into the briefest and most platonic of hugs. "Do you have anything special planned? Did you enroll in that summer program at the university I mentioned?"

The observership? No. Definitely not on the allowed list of summer activities.

She loved how he encouraged her and adored him even more for slipping the list of colleges with undergraduate pre-med programs inside her lab notebook. He was the one who'd told her about the highly competitive six-year medical school programs as well.

"Good-bye, Mr. Peterson," she said.

He finally released her. Perfect timing, too, since her breathing had already accelerated.

She glanced at the clock hanging over the doors leading outside as it counted down her fate. Less than an hour remained. She should stay and linger within the halls to memorize every detail. Those images would serve her well in the months to come, but staying meant risking unwanted conversation.

Although she remained a frustrating mystery to her peers, she didn't care. She had brushed off the advances of boys and kept those rare girls interested in befriending the geek girl an arm's length away for years. Friends were liabilities. A pretty girl, Elsbeth made certain she remained too school for cool. Her brain would determine her future, not her standing within the social hierarchy of an average high school.

Ashes to New

CHAPTER TWO

HOME.

THE WORD conjured many images. A home should be a place of light. A place of love. A place of sanctuary and hope. Home was where weary souls rested their heads as day deepened to night and slumber brought peaceful dreams. Home was a place to recharge and recuperate from the toils of a difficult day.

Elsbeth's home was located at a crossroads where reason fled and insanity took root.

The Tudor monstrosity, which the state foster care system assigned as her place of residence, dominated the middle of a three-lot spread at the end of a long cul-de-sac. The owner had purchased the lots on either side for the privilege of setting his home apart. Not that Clark Preston needed more space. It was the status that came with the message. He had not only wealth, but the power to flaunt it.

Despite everything the house embodied, Elsbeth looked forward to coming home for only one reason.

Her foster brother, Forest, was bouncing a soccer ball from knee to knee, his tall, lanky form a mess of spindly limbs too long for his growing frame. She called him her little Beanpole for good reason, but this last year, he'd truly started to sprout into the nickname. An odd bird, he had a quirky personality that hid a brilliant mind. She wasn't the only one with too few friends.

Forest glanced up, his shock of blond hair glowing in the afternoon sun. He let the ball drop where he kicked it back and forth in a blinding array of footwork. "Hey, Elz." He stopped his fancy footwork. The ball rolled a few short feet away until it came to a stop against the azaleas. He turned his gaze upon her, an old soul looking out from behind the palest blue she'd ever seen. "Guess it's officially summertime."

With a deep breath, she clutched her schoolbooks against her chest. Yes, it was summer, but she had the classics to keep her company. Melville, Shakespeare, and Austen would smooth out the dark times ahead.

"What are you doing outside?"

Forest was more of a computer geek than a jock. He was happiest with the glow of a Retina display lighting his room and stimulating his mind. Her foster brother didn't play video games. He made them. Self-taught in the language of code, Forest would tinker and create his escape while she read herself into one.

Forest jerked a thumb toward the house. "He called the maids," he said with a grimace. "We're having company."

Her stomach turned in knots. "Tonight?"

"Yeah, told me to let the maids in and then said to stay out of their way."

"Did he say who was coming?" *Please don't let it be the slobbery fat judge.*

With a shake of his head, Forest retrieved the ball and then drew her into a hug. He was tall enough for her to rest her head against his bony chest. When Forest had first entered her life five years ago, he'd been shorter than her, small and fragile. He was slowly becoming a man.

She leaned into his embrace, shaking.

He kissed the top of her head. "Elz, we'll get through it. We always do."

A tear leaked from the corner of her eye. She brushed it away. "But you know what he's like with company." She was

12

supposed to be strong for Forest, but the mention of visitors on the first night of summer had her trembling.

Pressing his lips against her forehead, he tugged her in tight. "It's a moment in time, my sweet Elz, but only a moment, and like everything else, it will pass."

Clark Preston was a demon she understood. She'd learned how to survive his trials and tests, but when he invited others to share in his appetites, her coping skills would struggle to keep up with the demands he placed upon her. And, while it would be easiest to lose herself within the insanity, she had Forest to protect—and one other.

Still naive, Forest believed in the possibility of a brighter future. He would be eighteen soon, and she would follow a few weeks later. Freedom beckoned, but first, she would have to endure senior year. She worried what would happen when faced with the possibility of graduation and a man who would refuse to let them go.

An accident had stolen her parents and separated her from a baby brother. Clark Preston held the knowledge of what happened to her brother. He used that power to command her obedience. Forest had lost his family to something much worse. Somewhere within their tragedies, they had found each other. Forest's resilience astounded her because he believed they would be delivered from the evil that filled their lives. Even when she'd held him on that very first night, when he'd been broken, battered, and left bleeding on the basement floor, Forest had believed. She hadn't had the heart to tell him the truth.

Neither of them would be escaping this hell.

The front door opened, and two cleaning ladies exited.

The older one walked over, her black-and-white maid uniform impressively immaculate after her labors. "We're all done," she said. "We couldn't get into the basement to clean. If your father wants us to clean down there next time, he'll need to remove the lock."

"Yes, ma'am," Forest said with a gulp, his grip around Elsbeth's shoulders tightening. "I'll be sure to tell him."

The women secured their gear in the cleaning van and pulled out of the driveway, waving as they drove off.

With a sigh, Elsbeth walled off her mind from what her body would soon face. That's the only way she survived. Forest said it all the time. *It's just a body, Elz. It's not you.* And she would believe that. To do otherwise meant facing insanity.

"Come on, Beanpole."

It was half past four. Clark Preston would be home within the hour.

"We have to prepare."

Forest followed Elsbeth inside.

The house had been dusted and polished to perfection. The marble floor of the foyer gleamed in the light from the chandelier. To the left, the wooden floor of the library glistened with fresh polish, and the line of Persian rugs leading down the main hall had been vacuumed and aligned to form a straight path.

A grimace pulled at Elsbeth's face as she stepped around the first rug in line. In less than an hour, she'd be kneeling in that spot.

Forest rushed ahead, heading to his bedroom in the back of the house. "Come, I want to show you a new game."

Hugging her books tight, Elsbeth picked her way down the hall. "I don't have time." Indeed, she would barely make it back to the foyer.

"It'll only take a second," Forest urged.

The eagerness in his eyes pulled at her heart, but with company coming over, she couldn't afford to make a mistake.

"I promise, I'll check it out tomorrow."

Forest understood even if he didn't like the answer. The oddity of his mind would allow him to switch on and off with much greater ease than she'd ever accomplished. For that small gift, she envied him. She would need all of the remaining time to get in the right headspace to make it through the night.

"Okay," he said.

"And you need to make sure you're prepared, too."

His mind might be strong, but of the two of them, his body would break before hers.

"Ugh, okay," he said with a dejected slump of his shoulders. "I'll get ready."

"Good." Elsbeth headed to her room.

With over six thousand feet of living space, conversations would echo and tumble through the house, bouncing off cathedral ceilings, amplifying whispers. The house was composed of three levels. The main floor held the usual suspects—a marble entry foyer, wood-paneled library, formal dining room, and a modern kitchen that opened up to the great room. There was the basement of course, a place where she and Forest spent far too much time. And of course, there was the second floor.

Her room occupied the left wing—a spacious second master living suite with a sitting room adjoining her bedroom, including a walk-in closet and a bathroom with a jetted tub and steam shower.

Forest's rooms were on the opposite side of the house. He'd been allowed to take over two bedrooms joined by a Jack and Jill bathroom. He would sleep in one bedroom while the other glowed with light from multiple computer monitors.

Neither of them ventured upstairs. In five years, she'd never set foot on the bottom step of the staircase leading up to Clark Preston's bedroom.

Quickly, she set about the task of removing unwanted leg, pubic, and underarm hair, using a brand-new razor to ensure the smoothest finish. With plenty of time to spare, she made a pass of her room, straightening up. Then, she returned to the foyer and knelt on the first prayer rug.

Forest joined her a few minutes later, taking position behind and to the right of her. "Hey, Elz, you forgot your collar."

She grabbed at her neck, a moment of panic overtaking her. A quick glance at the clock had her heart thumping.

"I'll get it," he said.

She rose and took off down the hall. "No, I'll get it."

Was that the throaty roar of the Porsche?

She sprinted back to her room. *And where was the collar?* It wasn't in the tray beside her bed or attached to the chain hanging from the headboard. *Shit, where had he left it last night?* Her search turned frantic as the seconds ticked by, and that was most definitely the garage door rising on its tracks. The rumbly sound transmitted through her wall. *Shit!*

Elsbeth gave up the search and raced back down the hall. Her bare foot twisted on the corner of the rug, flipping the woven wool over. Crashing to her knees, she assumed the position of greeting moments before the door leading from the garage opened. Forest widened his stance, clasping his hands behind his back and lowering his head, as required. She pressed her palms to the ground and bowed, touching her forehead to her knuckles.

Clark Preston's dark force rolled across the gap separating her from him and settled with a heavy presence on her shoulders. A dark gray Armani suit brushed the tops of his Salvatore Ferragamo dress shoes, and the firmness of his steps echoed in the expanse of the foyer.

Eleven steps—that was how many it took. Not ten, not twelve, but eleven. The number was precise and had been ingrained in her mind since she the age of twelve.

One…two…three…

Each thunderous sound snapped with the beating of her heart.

"Congratulations," he said.

Four…five…six…

Her heart beat against the cage of her chest, pumping adrenaline through her veins.

Elsbeth squeezed her eyes shut, packaging up the fragile pieces of her mind and locking them away. She eased her breathing, not daring to show any signs of fear. He would seize upon her weakness and exploit it, and she didn't need to give him an advantage, not when he held all the cards. This was a war she could not win. A battle of attrition, however, that she would endure.

Eleven came much too quickly, and the polished leather of his shoe brushed her forehead. "Give your daddy a kiss, little one."

Lifting her head, she brushed the top of his shoe with her lips. The ritual disgusted her, but as Forest had said, this was nothing but a channel of time. She would have to get from this moment to the next and through the one following that. That was the path they would take until morning came.

Survive. That was the goal.

Eventually, Clark Preston would tire and take to his rooms upstairs, and as he retired for the night, she would unlock those parts of herself she'd jealously guarded. All would be right.

If only she could find a way to make Clark Preston disappear forever and not merely for the span of a day…

Revulsion rippled through Elsbeth's body with the press of her lips against the fine Italian leather of Clark Preston's shoes. Everything about the man screamed power, control, domination, and terror, especially when he aimed his sick desires upon her and Forest. A rich man, he was deemed a perfect foster father, and the social workers loved that he preferred fostering older children. They saw his firmness as a strength to help troubled teens find their way through the system and into independent living.

In many ways, Forest's arrival had been both a blessing and a curse. He took pressure off the demands that had been placed upon her, but Clark Preston's carefully crafted threats would turn her hesitation to eagerness. Whatever it took to draw attention away from the scrawny little boy with perpetual tears in his eyes, she would manage.

And, with those memories swirling to the forefront of her mind, Clark Preston lowered himself into a crouch. As she suppressed a shiver, Elsbeth's breathing hitched. This wasn't the usual sequence of events. His slender but unforgiving index finger dug into the soft tissue beneath her jaw, forcing her head up. She lifted her eyes to meet the steel shimmering in his gaze while willing her body not to tremble at his touch.

"Little one," he said, "you forgot your collar. Tsk, tsk." The angle of his gaze cut over her shoulder, latching on to Forest standing at rigid attention. "Did you tell Elsbeth that we were having company?"

"Yes, sir." There was no hesitation in Forest's voice.

He couldn't protect her from the mistake. They both knew this, and to lie to Clark Preston was to invite punishment. Enough pain would come without either of them asking for more.

Clark Preston swept the hair off her nape. The flowing long strands brushed the expensive wool of the carpet. His fingers scraped against her skin, pebbling her flesh. "I am not pleased, little one."

She gritted her teeth. He was never pleased. Perfection was impossible. And forgetting her collar was a nearly unforgivable sin. Begging forgiveness would excite him, and for that reason, she said nothing, not that he'd granted her the right to speak. Her mouth had only one purpose, as far as he was concerned, and it wasn't to waste time with unnecessary words.

"It's a shame," he said with a sigh.

With her vision glittering behind a veil of unshed tears, the crystal of his watch flashed in her periphery.

"Our guests will be here at any moment. Now, my pets, where do you think we should entertain them?"

"I prepared the basement for you and your guests, sir," Forest said.

They had assigned tasks. Hers was to turn her body into a flawless tableau for Clark Preston's amusement. Forest's preparations weren't as extensive, but he was charged with setting up the basement each night. They would clean up afterward while Clark Preston stumbled upstairs to retire in his rooms.

The one saving grace in both their lives lay within the sanctuary of their rooms. For some reason, that space was inviolate. Not that Clark Preston couldn't call her out on a whim, but he never violated that space. When she was in her room, Elsbeth could relax.

He stood, towering over her, the gravity of his gaze suffocating. She couldn't look away, not until he gave permission.

His fingers tugged at his belt, loosening the buckle. "Well, my dear, I think ten strikes shall suffice, and then you will find your collar. In fact, just so you don't lose it again, you won't remove it for the rest of summer."

A whimper escaped her, and she nearly did beg. Wearing the collar wasn't an issue. It was a piece of leather, expensive as hell, and despite what it was used for, the collar was comfortable. It had been the words following his pronouncement that were the most damaging. *For the rest of summer*—those words sealed her fate. If he intended her to never take it off, there was no way she would be allowed outside.

The things that happened inside these walls never left them, and now, she'd be trapped without escape until the school year began again.

She'd tried once to reach out for help. The first week, when her caseworker had come for the obligatory checkup appointment for the newly placed child, Elsbeth had confided in the woman.

But the woman hadn't believed.

Instead of removing Elsbeth from the house, the social worker had expressed concerns to Clark Preston. The man was a lawyer with a silky tongue that could charm a snake. He'd convinced the woman that Elsbeth had fabricated the story because the new house intimidated her, and he'd asked if he could have another day to help Elsbeth work through her fears. That was the first time Elsbeth had spent a day immobilized in bed. Needless to say, when the social worker had returned, Elsbeth had retracted her wild story. Her voice had been contrite as she sealed her future.

Ten strikes?

He was letting her off easy, which served to heighten her fear.

What was he saving her for? Who was he saving her for?

CHAPTER THREE

WHILE A LIGHT punishment, ten strikes of his belt hobbled Elsbeth. She limped back to her rooms to search for the collar she would wear for the next three months. School was the one saving grace in life. He couldn't refuse her attendance. A few tears threatened to fall, but she wouldn't allow herself to cry. Tears were a waste of time, and with each breath, more time would pass.

After a thorough search, the collar was once again wrapped around her neck. It had fallen to the floor during her hasty cleaning spree, hidden between the nightstand and bed. Taking in a deep breath, she once again tucked the more fragile pieces of herself back into the darkest recesses of her mind. A brain vault was what she needed, a place where she could shove all the important pieces of herself and lock them away where they would be safe.

She'd left Forest alone with their foster father for far too long.

It wasn't hard to locate them. Music played, the soulful deep melody of Hans Zimmer's "The End" filled the air, setting the mood and lifting the fine hairs at her nape. Clark Preston's music would change with his sexual appetites. This choice proved worrisome because it placed Forest at the forefront of whatever was to come.

Her bare feet slapped on the travertine tiles of the kitchen. As she moved into the flowing open space of the kitchen and great room combination, the sight of Forest on his knees, harness already attached, confirmed her fears. Clark Preston had begun before his guests arrived. Her anxiety level tripled. He wasn't a man with great stamina, a blessing she counted many times. That he'd already engaged with Forest meant Clark Preston intended to be more of a spectator later tonight.

She approached the edge of the carpet, feeling the heat of Clark Preston's gaze settle upon her bare flesh. Lowering to her knees, she assumed the waiting pose, toes tucked under her legs. She sat straight, her attention locked on Clark Preston, so she wouldn't miss an unspoken command.

Forest faced her, his eyes full with pain. The harness pinched his flesh, and the collar constricted his breathing.

Elsbeth hated her helplessness to stop the abuse. Her palms slickened with sweat, and her gut twisted at the sight of the purplish hue overtaking Forest's face.

Someday, Clark Preston would go too far. The only thing saving them right now were the mandatory monthly check-ins by the caseworkers, not that he wouldn't be able to fabricate a story about how an awkward and troubled teen might have taken his life via strangulation.

A shudder rippled through Elsbeth as she counted out the seconds while Clark Preston sodomized her best friend. Forest bore the torment, eyes closed and jaw clenched, while she thought of something, anything, but what Clark Preston was forcing her to watch.

The moment stretched out, time slipping away, time standing still, time flowing with a mind of its own.

But time did pass until, finally, Clark Preston pulled out. With a yank of his trousers, he dressed himself and then sauntered into the kitchen. He'd yet to make eye contact with her, ignoring her as she knelt by the edge of the carpet.

He pulled out his cell phone and swiped at the screen. "Ah, perfect." His chuckle had her squirming. "Our guests will be here momentarily." Opening the fridge, he pulled out a beer and popped off the top. "Elsbeth, the judge will be joining us tonight. He was quite pleased last time and asked for you again."

The mention of the judge had her stomach heaving. Fortunately, Clark Preston had his back to her and didn't see her gagging, but her voice trembled, betraying her state of mind. "Yes, sir." The words barely made it past her lips.

Clark Preston came to stand beside her and grabbed her hair. Wrenching her head up, he forced her to face him. "He said you were a little distracted last time." His eyes cut to Forest, who was still kneeling in the middle of the great room, catching his breath. "Give the judge your undivided attention tonight."

That was the thing with Clark Preston. With a simple glance, he conveyed intent. Behave. Be endearing. Please the fat-assed judge. Failure would lead to consequence, and Clark Preston knew exactly how far she would go to protect Forest from the whip.

"Yes, sir." Her voice was remarkably steady now.

"That is good, little one." He turned his attention to Forest. "Clean up. I have a special surprise in store for you."

Forest opened his eyes. For the briefest moment, he held her gaze, but then his countenance splintered with the knowledge that he, too, would be participating in Clark Preston's games.

"Yes, sir." And, like her, Forest's voice held steady.

The doorbell's shrill call had her stiffening while Forest jumped. Clark Preston released his grip on her hair.

"Our guests have arrived." With a snap of his fingers, he commanded their attention. "Come."

The moment Clark Preston headed to the door, Elsbeth and Forest exchanged looks, taking strength in each other for what they would have to suffer through, but they didn't dare linger. Forest peeled off the harness, clambered to his feet and preceded her down the hall. She followed without hesitation.

Together, they knelt and waited while Clark Preston answered the door.

CHAPTER FOUR

THE MEET-AND-greet between the three men continued for an interminable length of time. Elsbeth's knees ached with only the thin wool of the rug to cushion her from the harsh marble floor.

Judge Henry Johnson kept glancing to where she knelt. Like Clark Preston, he, too, wore a suit. Plaid suspenders held his pants up, and atrocious argyle socks peeked out from beneath his trousers. He had flowing blond hair combed over the patch of baldness on top of his head. His beady brown eyes simmered with brewing lust, and his cock tented the expensive wool of his trousers.

She was going to get sick if she thought too hard about what would come next. The other man was a mystery, but Clark Preston greeted him like an old friend. That bothered her even more than the judge—or rather, the looks the newcomer gave Forest. The bottom drop out of her world. This new man was dangerous.

A polished individual, he wore cuff links that sparkled in the light cast from the chandelier overhead. Clark Preston shook the man's hand and exchanged pleasantries. A roll of cash passed between them.

Judge Johnson pulled out a stack of bills as well. Clark Preston lay the money down on the inlaid tile table, not bothering to count it. The cash would be locked in the safe behind the painting hanging over the massive mahogany desk in the library.

Fire burned in her cheeks and settled in her gut. That money stole her innocence one evening at a time.

"So, John, how was your flight?" Clark Preston asked.

Elsbeth breathed in through her nose and out through her mouth, trying to ease her anxiety with the slow breaths.

The newcomer ran long fingers through his mop of black hair, combing the waves into submission. "The flight was uneventful but long. You know how international travel can be."

"It wears you out, but I have the solution to that." He gestured to Elsbeth and Forest. "What do you think?"

The swell of pride in his tone soured her stomach. She and Forest were nothing more than objects to be used, and she hated that she allowed it. She despised how easily her will had been broken.

The strange man approached Forest. "Delectable, as you mentioned." He reached out and then withdrew, turning back to Clark Preston. "May I?"

Clark Preston nodded. "Of course. Forest, meet John Snowden. You're his for the evening. Elsbeth, once Judge Johnson is finished, you will serve Mr. Snowden as well."

"And I can do whatever I wish?" Snowden asked.

A shudder rippled down her spine.

"Within reason. You can't do anything that will permanently harm them, but that's stated in the contract."

"Of course." John Snowden traced the angle of Forest's jaw, tilting his head up. "I wouldn't dream of harming your property, but you did mention harder play."

Forest gave no reaction to the man's words, holding himself perfectly still.

Elsbeth's gut twisted and seethed. *Tonight would be difficult.*

The judge joined them, his step heavy and ponderous, and his fat hand pulled at her hair as he lifted it to sniff the strands. "You're in for a treat tonight, John. Clark's pets are incredibly well trained and obedient." He released her hair and marched past, no doubt headed to the liquor cabinet.

"The boy is a fine specimen," John Snowden proclaimed. "As is the girl. I can't wait to begin."

Clark Preston gestured down the hall. "Soon, but first, can I interest you in a drink? I have whiskey, scotch, or beer, if you prefer."

"Do you have Gentleman Jack?"

"I was betting you were a Jack fan. Two fingers, neat?"

John Snowden nodded. "Please."

The men left Elsbeth and Forest in the hall. In that sliver of a moment, Forest reached for her hand, curling his fingers around hers. They weren't allowed to speak, but everything that needed to be said was communicated in the squeeze of his fingers. He was there for her, as much as she would be for him.

Forest mouthed, *Time will pass.*

And, indeed, it would.

"Elsbeth!" Clark Preston's command snapped her to her feet. "Judge Johnson desires your attention."

She hustled to the great room, unsurprised to find the judge reclined in one of the two leather seats. A couch separated the two facing chairs. Clark Preston busied himself at the bar while the judge and John Snowden took residence in the camel-colored chairs.

Judge Johnson had his belt unbuckled and his trousers unzipped. There was no reason to ask for direction.

"Boy," John Snowden snapped, "come here."

While Forest moved to the spot in front of John Snowden, Elsbeth knelt before the judge and squeezed her eyes shut when the stench of him hit her nostrils. But she remembered Clark Preston's comment about her lack of enthusiasm, and she sought the quiet nothingness of her mind.

"No!" John Snowden struck Forest. "Not on your knees, boy. I want a good look at this cock I've heard so much about."

"Did I not tell you it was impressive?" Clark Preston's tone was filled with an odd emotion—part respect, part envy, but complete control.

She rushed to please the judge, bowing to her task with an enthusiasm she did not feel. The sooner she finished, the quicker she could move the attention off Forest and on to her.

"And the boy is how old?"

The judge's breathing deepened while anger bubbled within her and boiled to the surface.

Clark Preston preened his answer. "Seventeen."

"Well, that's convenient. And the girl?"

"The same."

John Snowden leaned forward, his appraisal intensifying. "Can you imagine what that cock will grow into?"

Elsbeth suppressed a shudder while listening to the men discussing Forest as nothing more than a piece of meat.

"Yes," Clark Preston said with a sigh. "Most impressive."

John Snowden leaned back. "Is he a virgin?"

"No, he's been fucked many times."

"That's not what I meant. Has he ever done the fucking?"

"You want him to fuck you?" Clark Preston failed to hide the surprise in his voice or the revulsion laced within.

John Snowden chuckled. "Not me, you fool. I want him to fuck the girl."

"Hmm…" Clark Preston's consideration of John Snowden's comment set Elsbeth's nerves on edge.

Those were not the words she needed to hear. Their foster father had done many things, but he'd never forced her and Forest into sexual contact before. One had always been a participant with the other held in reserve.

Who was this John Snowden to their foster father? A powerful man, to be certain, and the roll of bills he'd passed to Clark Preston far exceeded the judge's paltry stack. A thousand dollars was the usual fee for an evening's entertainment, but John Snowden had put much more than that in Clark Preston's hands.

"In fact," Clark Preston said with a drawl, "he's never fucked anyone."

Elsbeth squeaked when the judge palmed her head. "Focus, girl," he said with a snarl. "I'm almost there."

Gagging down her revulsion, she bit back a scream when he yanked on her roots and emptied himself down her throat with the force of his climax. The urge to wipe her mouth nearly overpowered her, but the weight of Clark Preston's stare settled heavily on her shoulders. With the powerful force of her will, Elsbeth sat back on her heels, obedient to a fault.

"What is his stamina like?" John Snowden leaned forward, his eyes focused on Forest's flaccid cock.

"He's young." Clark Preston lowered onto the sofa. "And well trained."

"I want to watch him fist that beast, and then I want to watch him fuck the girl. Hell, I want to fuck him while he fucks the girl." John Snowden's attention turned on her. "I want to fuck every hole—his and hers."

The judge chuckled. "Ambitious, are we?"

"That's what I'm paying for." He reached for Forest's cock but seemed to change his mind at the last minute. "And they'll obey?"

John Snowden's eyes cut to Elsbeth and made her cringe. "I'm very interested in this pair. You said they'd do whatever I wanted?"

"They will."

"Will they come or just go through the motions?"

Elsbeth's heart hammered beneath her breastbone. Fear surged in her veins. She was horrified by what this man intended.

Worse, shame filled her because she would do everything without question and without a fight.

"The girl has been trained. She comes like a fucking angel. The boy has not."

A sick revulsion crept deep into her bones. That he controlled her with such little effort twisted her from the inside out, but then he'd had five years to condition her responses.

"I might have some ideas on that." For the third time, John Snowden's attention shifted from Forest to her. His eyes narrowed, calculating and cold. "You mentioned a dungeon. I would very much like to see it."

"Of course."

John Snowden lifted his finger. "But a demonstration first." He snapped his fingers. "Girl, come here."

She couldn't move without Clark Preston's consent. And, even though it was foolish to hope, Elsbeth prayed her foster father would command her to stay in place.

But his mouth opened. His lips moved. His words condemned. "Little one, you will do as Mr. Snowden says."

Tears pooled in the corners of her eyes, but she wouldn't dare blink. He would know what that meant. He knew her every mood, and tears would hand over power because they betrayed weakness. She'd locked the core of her being in the darkest part of her mind, but John Snowden's demand had snapped all the locks, leaving her raw and breathless.

"Turn!" He slapped Forest's hip, twisting him until Forest faced her direction.

Her stomach sank—*please no*—but the steel in John Snowden's expression burned white hot.

He crooked a finger. "Come, girl." Pointing down, he indicated precisely where she was to kneel.

Forest's breathing hitched. His face paled, and the swell of his Adam's apple bobbed in his throat. Even his fingers fluttered against the sides of his thighs.

She wanted to escape, to turn around and rush right out the patio door, run until her feet bled and her lungs burned. But Forest would be left behind, a boy trapped with predators, and Clark Preston knew the one thing she did not. He knew the names of the people who'd adopted her baby brother. For these reasons, she crawled to the exact spot indicated by Snowden's finger.

The smile spreading on John Snowden's face had her insides a twisting mess. She nearly got sick but managed to control her body's revulsion for what would come.

Fear simmered in Forest's eyes. They'd been forced to do so much but never this.

A smile spread across John Snowden's face. "Now, this will be entertaining. We're going to find out how much stamina you have, little boy." His pupils dilated, the blackness swallowing the uninspired brown of his eyes. "Open wide, girl. I want to see him fill that pretty mouth of yours."

Ashes to New

CHAPTER FIVE

THE NIGHT BECAME a river of time, meandering toward morning but never seeming to quite get there. Hardly calm, the moments slipped by in a tumultuous raging torrent, buffeting Elsbeth, until dawn's cautious light finally cracked through the single small basement window. That sliver of light brought yawns to their tormentors and ushered the men upstairs to their beds. She and Forest remained locked downstairs, but she didn't care because the arrival of the sun meant one less day of summer stretching out before them.

She wasn't entirely certain about Forest's state of mind. He wasn't talking to her. *Had they broken him?* She feared that was the case. He was both too young and too fragile for John Snowden's merciless coercion. The things done to Forest had turned her stomach and soured her mouth. Even more heartbreaking, she had been one of the tools used to tear apart her precious Beanpole.

"Forest?" she asked. "Are you awake?"

His stillness worried her, and while she wanted nothing more than to wrap her arms around him, two things held her back. First, the steel bars of the cage limited her movement, but worse than not being able to hold and console him was the knowledge of exactly what touching him would do.

Forest slumped against the restraints holding him in place. The Saint Andrew's Cross creaked with his weight. The leather shackles groaned in protest. Sweat streaked his skin, and his golden locks hung limp where they dragged against his shoulders. His head dipped low, his chin brushing his chest, and his knees sagged, forcing his shoulders to bear the majority of his weight.

Whether from dejection or exhaustion, he didn't answer. He'd stopped speaking hours ago.

His entire body bore the evidence of the evening's abuse. Cane and whip marks marred his flesh, the visual display both wretched and terrifying.

Surges of testosterone hadn't done him any favors. He had bucked authority when he should've remained silent. It hadn't lessened Clark Preston's plans. Forest's resistance had done the opposite and spurred the men to tear into him until he gave in and begged for whatever they desired.

Confined inside the small cage, Elsbeth's body ached—not from the aftereffects of implements aimed at her flesh, but from her cramped conditions.

"Forest," she called out, "please answer me."

A moan escaped him, and his head rolled to the side, but he didn't answer. He was either unable or unwilling, and she prayed for the first. If he were ever unwilling to speak to her, she wouldn't want to live. Forest was her lifeline. He would keep her spirits up during the darkest of times. Perhaps now, it was her turn to do the same for him.

Shifting her weight to her left hip did little to relieve the aching in her limbs. Slowly, she reached out and stroked the cold steel. The metal stung her flesh but warmed slowly stealing her body heat as she palmed the unforgiving steel. "It's not your fault." She sniffed to hold back the tears. "You can't let him win."

He groaned and pulled himself up until he could bear his weight. "Elsbeth," he said with an agonized sigh, "I'm sorry."

The first night she'd met him, they were twelve, less than a month's difference in their ages. She'd held him until morning. Sodomized, broken, and bleeding, Forest had been given a stern introduction to his new home, and with a whip, Clark Preston had taught him what would happen to the little girl he now called his foster sister if he disobeyed.

"Don't let him win, Beanpole."

His head sagged from side to side, ponderous in its movement. "The things I did—"

"Weren't your fault." *Shoot, the things she'd done to him were worse.*

"I need you, Bean." She tried to portray confidence, but her need for his strength tunneled right through her words.

His head snapped up. The agony etched into his proud features revealed deep cracks in his control. "I'm sorry. I'm so sorry."

As was she, but they would get through this. They always got through it.

"We have each other, Bean." *They'd always have each other.* "Don't let them take that away. Don't disappear, not when I need you the most."

"Snowden is spending the summer with us."

Yes, she had heard the men talking. Clark Preston had spoken of John Snowden moving into the guest room on the upper level.

But for the whole summer?

"I love you," she said. *What else could fill the emptiness stretching between them?*

"I love you, too," he answered. "But I can't take another night of…of…of that."

"Do what you've always told me to do. Pack up everything important, and lock it up where they can't find it. It's a body, Forest. It's only a body."

Forest's icy-blue eyes turned up to focus on the door leading to freedom.

The lock turned.

She gripped the bar, leaning forward, as if that would give her a better view. The landing wasn't visible from where she crouched. The stiffening in Forest's frame told her everything she needed to know.

He had returned.

Clark Preston descended the half flight of stairs into the basement, his steps sure and determined. *Light even?* The anticipation in his tread raised alarm bells in Elsbeth's mind. Something was different, and that didn't bode well.

Their guardian paused before Forest, taking a measured assessment. After devouring Forest with his eyes, Clark Preston then caressed Forest's skin with his knuckles.

"You are miraculous," he said with a hint of awe. "I admire your strength."

Forest hung his head, pulling deep breaths in and out of his lungs. He didn't speak. He wouldn't, not until commanded. Elsbeth feared what would happen if he did. *Could Forest stand much more?* It would break him; of that, she was certain.

Bending her legs beneath her, she assumed the pose for greeting, hands pressed to the floor, forehead touching the backs of her hands. The entire cage shifted with her intent, doing exactly as she'd hoped. Clark Preston's heated gaze turned her way. And, while her stomach trembled with what would come next, she cheered for the result. Forest would sit this one out.

Only Forest didn't sit. Clark Preston forced him to remain on the Saint Andrew's Cross. When his legs buckled, he groaned against what must have been tremendous pain.

Clark Preston came to the cage, released her, and drew her to the far corner of the room. "We're going to try something, my pet."

******

It was noon before she was set free.

Hours of screaming had made her throat bleed. The forced orgasms had taken a different toll. Clark Preston's face had filled her mind and commanded her performance. When she'd failed, he had attacked Forest with a cane until she begged to be allowed another chance to come.

Pleased with her progress, Clark Preston left her with instructions to release Forest. It was Saturday, and they had the rest of the day off but were warned that Sunday would bring more guests.

She released Forest, and he slumped into her waiting arms. He could barely walk.

"Come," she said. "Let's get you cleaned up."

He moaned. "I can't do this anymore."

"You will."

He had to because she couldn't do it alone. Maybe that made her selfish—to want someone to share in the misery that permeated every painful breath. It had to mean she was a horrible person. *But how could she think otherwise?*

She took Forest into her bathroom because she had a tub.

"Why are you bringing me in here?"

"It's easier to help you in here."

"I can take a shower in my own bathroom."

"You're not even capable of supporting your weight, Bean."

His entire body was covered in dried sweat and crusty secretions. His rank smell inundated her nostrils and forced her to breathe through her mouth.

"I don't need your help."

His entire body shook as she held him. Getting him into the Jacuzzi tub took effort on both their parts, and it didn't help that they were still naked from the evening's activities.

Forest flinched every time she readjusted her hold. He pulled away when she wrapped her arm around him to steady him. He refused her grip when she tried to help him sit in the tub.

Hesitant to touch or terrified to be touched? There was little she could do about that.

He needed a bath, and he wasn't strong enough to do it himself.

The water coming out of the faucet was cold, and he hissed when it splashed his feet and lower legs. The water did warm, and with the filling of the tub, tension eased in his body.

She took the soap from the shower. Opening the cabinet, she retrieved a clean washcloth. When she returned to Forest, the water filled half of the tub. He had his head resting against the back of the tub, slipping down to submerge as much of his body as possible. Tension tugged at the corners of his closed eyes and reflected in the tightness of his jaw.

Crouching, she positioned herself on the edge of the marble step. "Do you want me to put on the jets?"

He cracked one eyelid and gave a shake of his head. "I'm good."

"Is it too warm?" She leaned over and tested the temperature.

"It's perfect. In fact, can you make it a little hotter?"

Making the adjustments, she dipped the washcloth into the water to wet it and then folded the soap inside. Reaching out, she pressed the washcloth to his upper arm.

Forest jumped. His eyes flew wide open, and his entire body shifted away.

She withdrew her hand. "Sorry, I didn't mean to surprise you."

His large hand took the washcloth. "I got this. Maybe just let me sit for a bit?"

"You might fall asleep."

"If I go under the water, I'm pretty sure I'll wake up." He held his body rigid, crossing his arms over his chest.

"Are you okay?"

The muscles of his jaw clenched. "I will be."

But was that the truth? Would either of them ever be okay? And, when Clark Preston went too far, what would happen? What would it take to free her and Forest? There weren't too many answers to that question. Would she be strong enough? Could she?

When she glanced at Forest, the answer materialized. She'd be strong enough for whatever it took.

Ashes to New

CHAPTER SIX

CLARK PRESTON'S CONTROL, while powerful, paled next to the deliberate practice of John Snowden.

Over the first week of summer, he shaped and honed Elsbeth's responses, using cruelty and coercion mixed with reward. The reward was the one thing she cared about most—him not touching Forest. Master John, as she was forced to address him, applied his sadistic principles to condition her responses. Her body broke under his demands, but even more damaging was how he settled himself deep within the crevices of her mind. His dark commands would whisper through her dreams, turning nightmares into reality with the coming of dawn.

One week into summer, it was Sunday, seven long days after his arrival. The door to the dungeon remained closed but only because Master John had a flight to catch. Elsbeth and Forest would soon be free of his calculating manipulation, and she wept with relief.

Her gaze kept cutting to the clock on the mantel, watching the minutes tick by.

"How long this time, John?" Clark Preston wrapped his fingers in Elsbeth's hair and let the long strands slip through his grip.

He was in a gentle mood, and she stilled, terrified the wrong movement would make all that change.

The same could not be said of Master John. He'd been especially horrid this morning. She'd been able to save Forest from most of his attention, but he had wanted a parting gift and brought out the whip. Forest had continued to resist, and she didn't understand why.

As his body matured into that of a man, he would become harder to control, if not impossible. If she'd considered that possibility, Clark Preston had, too, and fighting wasn't helping anyone. For now, Forest's gangly body and lack of coordination kept the balance of power firmly seated where it had always been.

"Negotiations on this one are tricky," Master John said. "With so many agencies involved, the legal land mines are impressive. I anticipate a few weeks, maybe longer." He gripped the chain attached to Forest's collar, pulling Forest's face tighter against his own lap. "I'm going to miss your boy."

Clark Preston chuckled. "As I'm certain, he'll miss you. It's been quite...educational, having you visit."

Master John released the chain and grabbed Forest's head, his large hands palming Forest's ears, controlling the up and down motion. His hard stare latched on to what Forest was doing with his mouth, and his jaw clenched with the sensations Forest drew from his body.

Elaborately knotted rope secured Forest's arms to his back, and a webbing of intricate ties bound his legs, forcing him into a precarious position on his knees. Heavy welts covered his back, marks from a whip endured less than an hour ago. A cut over his hip, angry and raw, had finally stopped bleeding.

Elsbeth laid her cheek against Clark Preston's thigh and closed her eyes.

"And your plans upon your return?"

Master John tilted his head back. His jugulars stood in relief over the strain of muscles in his neck. Elsbeth entertained a brief fantasy involving a sharp knife. With growl he released, and then he pushed Forest away and tucked his cock behind the zipper of his expensive suit. Forest wobbled, desperately trying to maintain his balance.

Icy revulsion rippled through Elsbeth's body.

Clark Preston played with her hair, pulling on the strands. As he stood, he brought her from her knees to her feet. "You should say good-bye." He palmed her neck, steering her toward Master John.

Forest lost the battle with his balance and fell over onto his side. A whoosh of air escaped with a grunt. Still heaving, his chest billowed in and out with each breath. While he had to be in excruciating pain, he remained still, not resisting the rope binding him.

"Good-bye, Master John." Keeping her voice contrite challenged every fiber of her being, but with a glance at Forest's struggle, she found the strength she desperately needed. Unsure as to what was expected in a farewell, Elsbeth dropped to her knees. As with the ritualized greeting, she stretched out and placed her lips on the top of his shoe.

Master John's gentle chuckle gutted her. "Ah, my sweet pet. I'll spend my evenings thinking of the deliciousness of your screams and fisting my cock to memories of your moans calling out for me. You're a true treasure and well worth what I paid."

She remained silent, maintaining her pose of obeisance.

He lowered himself to a crouch, cupped her jaw, and tilted her head up. "I'll be back. In the meantime, Clark will continue your training. You have much to learn."

Her heart skipped a beat. Clark Preston was a horrible man, but John Snowden was the true monster. *Did this mean his presence would be a recurring thing?*

"She's shaking," Clark Preston said as he stepped close. "Impressive."

"You're the one doing an impressive job. I only laid down the finishing touches. But she still needs work before I take possession." Master John released her chin.

Blood drained from her face, and her heart slammed against the cage of her chest. She dropped her chin, letting the long curtain of her hair hide her shock. She could barely breathe as his words tumbled in her head. *No! She had a future planned. Clark Preston had stolen her childhood, and now, this man planned on stealing her entire life?*

"You know what it takes and use the boy to reinforce her training. I don't want her getting used to coming only with the wand."

"Have you made a decision about the boy?"

"He's a fun distraction, but our arrangement is only for the girl. If you have difficulties with placing him, I might have a friend or two in mind."

Elsbeth pressed her forehead against the floor. *What arrangement? What the hell was he talking about?*

CHAPTER SEVEN

SUNDAY.

THE DAY was supposed to be a one of reflection. A day of prayer. And, like each breaking dawn, it was time to renew and refresh one's soul. Sunday was meant to prepare for the challenges of the coming week.

It wasn't meant to be was a day of torment.

Elsbeth prayed to end her existence. Several times, she plotted the best way to end her life. Strangulation seemed to be the most effective option. Clark Preston kept plenty of rope in the basement, and the overhead beams were sufficiently high. Knives terrified her. Even if slitting her wrists would bring a swift end, it would be messy. Overdosing? Not an option. She had no access to drugs and had been confined to the house for the duration of the summer.

And Forest? What would he do without her? She couldn't leave him behind, but would she dare take him?

She wanted to scream. She wanted nothing other than to lift her face to the heavens and belt out her misery.

Instead, she remained in position, impotent and weak, while Master John collected his luggage and departed the house. Her prayers for respite went unanswered because Clark Preston marched back into the great room and commanded her to release the rope binding Forest. They were then both ordered to the basement.

The next few hours, Clark Preston refined the techniques he'd learned from Master John. As evening chased the sun under the blanket of night, Elsbeth struggled to catch her breath. She couldn't handle any more, and even worse, Clark Preston had developed a newfound fascination with voyeuristic sex.

He directed their every move, forcing them into the most intimate embrace, every inch explored, every passage breached. She kept her eyes closed during most of it, her insides a writhing mess of fractured emotions, but Forest's reaction was much more concerning. While his body responded to the physical stimuli, his mind faded, growing distant.

During the bleakest times, he had always been the one to provide an anchor, curling his fingers around hers. That touch had given her hope. He'd fortified her strength by lending his.

But, the last three times she'd reached for his hand, moments when Clark Preston could not see the tender connection, Forest had withdrawn.

Forced into an intimacy neither of them desired, the one thing she needed was what Forest withheld—his fingers gripping hers. Without him to tell her it would be okay, Elsbeth's mind spiraled into darkness. Her vow to survive splintered. Hope fled. Nothing mattered. Her body worked on autopilot, responding to Clark Preston's demands, while she disappeared.

Time passed. It was the one thing Clark Preston could not control. They missed lunch and suffered through dinner, but eventually, the bright summer sky shining through the tiny basement window turned gray and then darkened to ink black.

Finally, Clark Preston rose from his chair. "You may go to your rooms."

She cleared her throat and dared a question. "Sir, may I prepare a meal before you turn in?"

He turned his wrist, glancing at the time. "That would be nice, little one." He patted her head and walked to the stairs. At the top of the landing, he turned, glancing down. "Master John is very taken with you."

"Sir, may I ask a question?"

His eyes narrowed. "Not one you already know the answer to."

His gaze held hers for an eternity, and she found the answer held within the fondness of his expression. He would miss her, which meant she would be leaving.

But what would happen to Forest? And when was her departure scheduled?

******

Elsbeth knocked on the door to Forest's computer room. He hadn't been in his bedroom, unusual for a boy who scheduled his sleep with religious zeal—or at least during those times when he was allowed to do so. Perhaps that explained his dogged determination to achieve a minimum of seven-point-five hours of sleep every night.

"Elz?" he called out.

Why he'd questioned who was knocking at his door surprised her. Clark Preston wouldn't have bothered with the courtesy.

She pulled at the leather band encircling her neck. While she hated the collar, she did give a moment of thanks to Clark Preston for the well-crafted leather. It fit perfectly and stunned her in those rare moments when she forgot its presence.

"Forest?"

"Come in."

He sat in front of a bank of computer screens—gifts earned through compliance and jealously guarded by his continued good behavior. The screen in front of Forest glowed with lines of blue text. Squinting, she couldn't make out intelligible words and wondered what project held his attention today. *His game?*

On the last day of school, a day that seemed like years in the past rather than a week ago, he'd asked her to look at his new game. With the arrival of Master John and all that had ensued, she hadn't had a chance to make it back to his rooms. Master John's visit had sent Forest into withdrawal. She tried to give him the space he needed, but she missed her Beanpole. She craved the easy interaction they'd always maintained in those few moments between waking, school, and the arrival of their foster father.

The screen to his left was an expanded display, easily the size of two monitors combined. It held a graph of ragged up and down lines. The screen to his right had a movie playing, some action flick involving a most unrealistic car chase through crowded city streets. He had the sound muted. One more monitor completed his workstation, elevated above the main working screen, one of his older games playing.

"Working on your game?"

"Nah, I'm trying something out." He tapped the screen to the left. "I'm working on an algorithm."

"For what?"

"Commodities and stocks. I'm trying to figure out the pattern." With a flick of his mouse, his game disappeared. He pulled up a trading website. "I think I'm close."

The speed with which his fingers flew over the keys astounded her, and she considered herself a fast keyboarder.

Elsbeth liked to think of herself as smart. Top of her class with straight As, she barely had to work to make good grades. Her chemistry teacher, Mr. Peterson, had said her GPA would open doors for her. With scholarship money available to children in the foster care system, she hoped to pay for college. Many had said she had been blessed with brilliance, yet her abilities paled when compared to her most treasured friend.

Forest's mind operated on another plane than the rest of humanity. He perceived the world in subtly different patterns, making it difficult for him to interact with his peers. Socially, he was a mess, an awkward outsider crippled by his uniqueness. Oddly, he struggled to maintain the Cs demanded by their foster father. It didn't make sense why he failed when he should be leading the class.

"You're trading? Is that even allowed?"

"I've been trading since I was fifteen, but there aren't any laws against it—as long as you're over fourteen."

"Where did you get the money?"

Neither of them was allowed anything more than what was required for their school lunches. They depended on Clark Preston for everything.

His fingers stopped tapping, and his body stilled.

"Forest?"

"It's our money, Elz." He turned around to face her. "We earned it."

The money was tainted, paid to steal their innocence, but that didn't mean it belonged to them.

"How did you—"

"I cracked the lock. It's a simple combination. Hardly a challenge."

"When?"

"When he was sleeping."

Oh, that had been a dangerous move.

"If he ever finds out…"

Her words of warning were wasted on Forest. He'd already taken the cash.

"Relax. He'll never know."

"He will."

Clark Preston knew everything.

"Don't worry; I put it all back."

She pressed a palm to her belly and tried to stop the sinking sensation happening in her gut. "Why did you take it, only to put it back?"

"I needed seed money for the investments." He tapped the display with the jagged red line. "Once I pulled off enough profit, I put the money back in the safe. He's never going to know because nothing is missing."

The entire e-commerce trading market baffled her desire to make sense of it. Her mind gravitated toward biological sciences. Her ultimate goal was to go to medical school, working toward a career where she could cure the sick and heal the wounded. That first night when she'd held Forest's broken, battered, and bleeding body, she'd made a vow to learn how to fix people.

"And how is it going?"

His lips firmed into a thin line. "Not as well as it could be. It's a struggle."

She crept closer, cautious about invading his personal space; it was yet another change in their relationship after Master John's visit. Leaning over his shoulder, she peered at the screen. A balance of three thousand dollars showed in an account. The line below held seventeen hundred. The one below that held seventy-two hundred.

But the line at the bottom made her gasp.

"Fifty thousand! How much money did you take?"

He shrugged. "I needed ten to start."

And, now, he had well over...

She added up the accounts, rounding as she went. *Fifty...fifty-three...fifty four...fifty five, sixty one! No...nearly sixty two thousand sat in his online accounts.*

"How long have you been at this?" *And why had he never mentioned it?*

50

"I wanted it to be a surprise. I didn't know if I could make it work, but I'm figuring out a rhythm."

"Make what work?"

He stretched his hand out but withdrew at the last minute. The shakiness of his fingers betrayed his unease.

Forest hadn't touched her outside of what was required in the basement. She missed her Beanpole hugs.

"I wanted to give you a graduation present." He tapped the bottom line of the screen. "You'll need a lot more, of course. Medical school is crazy expensive, and this six-year program you want isn't any cheaper. I almost have enough to cover the cost of the first year. I'm hoping to pay for it all by the time we graduate."

Her heart ripped open upon hearing his plans, followed shortly by tears bursting from the corners of her eyes. "You want to pay for my school?"

She shivered with the looming weight of what Master John had intimated before he left. She wasn't naïve; she understood his intent for her future.

Forest rose from his seat and gathered her into a hug. "I won't let him take you, Elz. We'll stop him. Whatever it takes." He brushed back her hair and kissed her forehead. "A healer is waiting inside your heart. And a kick-ass doctor is swirling in that brain of yours. I won't let them steal your future."

Releasing her, he turned back to his monitors and lowered himself into the chair. "No matter what it takes."

Ashes to New

CHAPTER EIGHT

IT TOOK ANOTHER month and a half before Master John returned. Whatever business he'd had overseas kept him out of their home for the majority of the summer, but time had marched on, relentless and determined.

Soon, Elsbeth and Forest found themselves on their knees, waiting on his arrival.

School would start in a couple weeks. Their senior year.

At eighteen, they would be legally eligible to exit the foster care system. One question remained though. *After everything he'd done, would Clark Preston let them leave?*

An arrangement had been struck between Master John and Clark Preston. Forest didn't seem to be included in the deal. *How did he plan on controlling her without the threat of hurting Forest?* She was missing something. *And what did Clark Preston have planned for Forest?*

Clark Preston sat in the library, working on his case files. She had no idea what kind of lawyer he was. She didn't care. And it never came up in idle conversation, not that the three of them engaged in chitchat.

She needed to focus on the here and now. Slow her breathing. Calm her heart. Tackle the nerves fluttering in her belly and channel that energy into something useful. Control what she could and worry about the rest later.

To her left, Forest's deep breathing pulsed into the air separating them.

When she dared to stretch her hand to soothe him, he jerked away. His aversion to her touch had only intensified over the intervening weeks.

She'd barely seen him this past month. During the day, he would disappear inside his computer room, and at night, he'd close the door to his bedroom. He'd said he was working on his project, but she understood.

Forced into intimate contact nearly every night, Forest was avoiding her.

Clark Preston would pose them, filming his nonstop narrative direction. She and Forest never spoke as they moved like the puppets they had become.

Focus!

Master John would be here soon.

A chill ripped through her body, and she fisted her fingers tight until her nails cut into her palms. Her mind was a raw and ravaged mess, and she was failing to package the important bits and squirrel them away. She needed to find her center if she was going to survive the night.

A rustle of paper trickled out from the library. Clark Preston had finished working on his latest case. His leather chair creaked as he rose, and then his steps filled the silence, echoing against the walls and bouncing off the ceiling to lodge deep in her chest. He came to a stop before them, the weight of his power settling heavily on her shoulders.

"Not long now. Master John has a treat for you, boy."

Elsbeth's insides twisted. With her head pressed to the backs of her hands, she squeezed her eyes shut and prayed.

******

Whatever Master John had planned for Forest never materialized. Master John had apologized, saying it would be another couple of weeks.

Elsbeth sought answers and found none, her mind fearful and full of too many what-ifs.

With the arrival of Master John, daily activities commenced downstairs. Forest endured brutal beatings while she drowned in forced pleasure. Her mind learned to respond to delivered commands, and her body bent to Master John's will. Days ran into one another, blurring lines and erasing boundaries. Forest grew even colder and detached, rarely speaking in the few spare moments they found themselves unmolested.

During the endless summer, he'd spend hours in the basement, alone with Master John. When released, Forest would retreat to his rooms. She'd knock on the door, wait, but her pleas would remain unanswered. They suffered, apart from each other. He'd barely look at her and never in her eyes. They wouldn't touch outside the basement, his body conditioned to respond in a way he couldn't process.

They endured together. Separated, they were falling apart.

She picked up the pieces as best as she could.

The days churned by.

Elsbeth feared for the future, but never gave up trying to reach Forest.

She knocked on Forest's door. "Come on! Let me in."

While they had locks on the doors, they weren't permitted to use them. So, when she twisted the knob and found her entry barred, Elsbeth gaped. This was not good. If Clark Preston found Forest locking his door…well, that couldn't happen.

She rapped on the wood and lowered her voice, frantic now more than ever to reach him. "Forest?"

No response.

"Forest!"

A chair scraped over the tile floor, but no other sound reached her ears.

"Is something wrong, my pet?" The liquid tone of Master John's voice poured into her soul and shut it down.

Where had he come from?

With her hand on the doorknob, she froze.

He invaded her personal space and tucked a strand of hair behind her ear. With the soft press of his lips against the angle of her jaw, he brushed her arm. "What's the matter? Why do you run to him when you have me to turn to?"

Because Forest was safe.

A trail of kisses traveled down the curve of her neck, Master John lapping and nibbling at her collarbone.

Gripping her wrist, he pulled her hand off the doorknob and pressed it to the hardness of his shaft. "I find myself in need, my pet. What should we do?"

"Forgive me, Master John."

Everything with him was, *Forgive me, Excuse me, I'm sorry.*

She hated him with a burning passion. Lowering to her knees, she prepared to offer her mouth.

He held her in place. "No, my pet, not like that."

"To the basement?"

She'd spent the morning with him—being trained, as he called it. The bulk of the day, she'd been free to roam, which meant she'd shut the door to her rooms and read one of her books. In those few hours, she'd lived a different life and dreamed of another future.

He shook his head and drew her away from the closed door. "No, my pet. I have something special in mind."

The room spun. His surprises never boded well for her.

"Ye-yes, sir."

With a hardening of his tone, he made her blood chill. "Never sir. I'm your master."

The words landed on her sluggish mind without the impact he seemed to want. Her silence had him pulling her through the house, down the long hall, and into the foyer. When he approached the steps leading upstairs, she dug in her heels. Five years in this house, and she'd never ventured up there.

"Please, Master John, can we not go to the basement?"

"I'm offering my bed to you, and you want to go there? Do you know the privilege in sharing my bed?"

Oh, dear God, no.

For whatever reason, Clark Preston had left the sanctity of their rooms inviolate. No matter what happened during the day or in the evenings when he came home, she always had the security of her bed, and now, Master John wanted her, up there, and in his bed.

A strangled cry erupted from her throat, and she did the unthinkable. She refused.

Elsbeth tugged out of his grip, staggering, while the room spun, and a buzzing filled her head.

Master John slapped her cheek, his shout nothing but unfiltered noise.

She wouldn't go. Not up there. Never there.

Movement blurred in the periphery of her vision. Forest advancing at a run. She fell, crying out as she landed on unforgiving marble.

Fury boiled in Forest's expression. He swung at Master John, his fist moving too slowly. Gangly. Awkward. Forest missed. Master John grabbed Forest's wrist, using momentum to pull him forward and down. Forest landed in a heap, his head cracking on the marble, and his body going still.

"No!" She scrambled to Forest, hugging his limp form, as tears poured down her cheeks.

"What the hell is all the racket about?" Clark Preston's stern voice silenced her cries.

Master John yanked her off Forest. "Don't you ever disobey again." He turned to Clark Preston. "That one is a liability. Put him down."

He lifted her off her feet. Kicking and screaming, she was carried downstairs.

"You'll discover what happens when you displease your master."

Rage filled her, burning from the inside out, and she erupted with seething anger. "You're not my master. You'll never be my master."

He held her chin in the hardness of his embrace. His searing gaze stole her breath. "Since the day you stepped foot in this house, I have been your master. I will always be. And I'll do whatever I want with you."

CHAPTER NINE

FOR MOST PEOPLE, basements were dark places where order grew into disorganized chaos with the storing and sorting of unwanted things.

Clark Preston's basement was something else entirely. Finished. Soundproofed. Wired to provide whatever sound or lighting effect he desired. From the harsh light of fluorescents to the amber glow of candlelight, he could match lighting, sound, and mood, and Elsbeth could prepare her mind for what would follow.

Padded flooring covered the cement floor, the one concession he allowed his foster children, who spent too many hours on their knees. Rows of hangers and hooks lined the walls, and these were loaded with implements meant to inflict nothing but pain.

A bed. A cage. And several benches.

But the centerpiece had to be the Saint Andrew's Cross, which dominated the room.

Master John did not take her to the cross, and she had a suspicion as to why. Instead, he led her toward the back of the room where he trussed her arms over her head against the wall.

Ragged and gasping, she couldn't collect enough air. Blackness edged her vision, tunneling her sight. Pins and needles poked at her fingertips and buzzed at the edges of her lips.

"You are and always will be mine." The heat of Master John's breath warmed her neck and sent shivers rippling down her spine. "You have been from the moment you arrived. Trained for me, kept for me, until you were ready to leave *with me*. You don't understand, but you will."

Her whimper was met with a hard yank of her hair, snapping her head back. He cracked her ass with his palm, raising her up to her toes with a shriek pulled from her lungs.

"You will obey. You will please. You'll do everything I command." He punctuated each word with a strike of his hand, leaving her breathless and in agony.

Tears poured down her cheeks, and her nose ran.

"We leave in a week, my love," he said with a rumbling low chuckle.

She stilled.

Leave? Her senior year would begin in less than two weeks.

"Now, that got your attention."

His hand rubbed where he'd struck her ass, and she hissed against the intimate touch.

Permission to talk had not been granted, but she didn't care. "What do you mean, leave?"

"You know exactly what I mean."

"I have school, and my caseworker—"

"Has already signed off. Funny what people will do for money. It's been arranged."

"I won't."

She couldn't leave Forest.

"It's not a choice."

Without Forest, Master John had no leverage.

"I'll run away. You can't keep me."

He laughed. "Oh, my pretty pet, you don't want to do that."

The basement door creaked, opening slowly.

"Give me a hand," Clark Preston called out. "The little shit's heavy as fuck."

With a gasp, she twisted away from the wall, but Master John pressed her shoulder, holding her in place. "Face the wall, or I'll hood you. I'm a patient master, but don't test me. The more you obey, the easier things will be."

She whimpered, "Please don't hurt him." Racking deep sobs chopped at her words, making them incoherent.

Desire to turn and see what the men were doing to Forest overwhelmed her, but fear kept her nose pressed to the hard concrete.

"Don't move, my sweet. I need to help Clark."

He left her trembling against the wall, her arms stretched overhead, bound and secured. She leaned her forehead against the wall and slowed her breathing, struggling to listen.

They'd been in similar situations before. They'd get out of this one, too.

"Thanks," Clark Preston said. "Fucker is getting bigger every year."

"He's skinny," Master John said.

"Won't be for long."

"How can you be so sure?"

"I've seen kids like him before," Clark Preston said with a grunt. "Give him a few years to pack on muscle, and your buddies will be making hand over fist, fighting him."

Fighting? Her mind conjured images of illegal fighting rings. She'd read about them in books. *But those men volunteered, didn't they?*

And that line of thought took her down dark and deadly paths. If she could be sold to Master John, Forest could meet with a similar fate.

But why fighting? Didn't they know his gentle nature?

"I give him less than a year." Master John's offhand comment had her whipping her head around.

Forest hung limply. His arms and legs dangled. The two men carried him to the Saint Andrew's Cross, and while Clark Preston secured the belt around Forest's waist, Master John caught her staring. His head shook, disappointment weighing heavily in his gaze. He said nothing, shifting his hold on Forest, while Clark Preston bound Forest's arms and legs to the cross.

"I think my little bird doesn't understand."

Clark Preston huffed with the effort of strapping Forest to the beams of the cross. "Huh?"

Transfixed within the intent of Master John's soulless eyes, Elsbeth couldn't turn away. She should. If she cared about her safety or even that of Forest's, she would resume the position he'd put her in, but she couldn't. She met and measured her master's determination, and she shattered.

With Forest trussed up where he wouldn't fall, Master John released him. He sauntered over, each step slow, measured, and ferocious. His eyes cast left, searching, and then he diverted left. From the top of a bench, he picked up a black piece of fabric. A hood.

"A lesson, little girl." His voice dripped with danger. "Never test my resolve to do exactly as I've promised."

With a gulp, Elsbeth tried to swallow the lump forming in her throat. Her eyes widened as he lifted the hood.

As she shook her head, her entire body trembled. "Please, don't!"

His sickly sweet cologne filled her nostrils, and she gagged.

"Clark and I need a moment with your foster brother. Don't make me come over here again."

The hood descended over her head, shutting out light and muffling sound.

He kissed the angle of her shoulder. "You may beg for forgiveness later."

******

Later came quite some time, well, later.

During the endless moments before, Forest's shrieks had pierced the air to knife directly into her heart, twisting and shredding it to pieces. As she was shrouded within the darkness of the hood, her imagination conjured the worst images, and based upon his screams, she feared her guesses were all too accurate. Nevertheless, time marched forward. The men tired of Forest, leaving him sobbing on the basement floor.

Broken? Most definitely. Bleeding? She hoped not.

Sometime ago, the men had taken him off the Saint Andrew's Cross. He'd been roughly used since then.

The booted tread of feet approached, and she stiffened, preparing for the promise Master John had made. It was her turn.

How to minimize the damage? Her mind churned and left her with nothing.

Persist and endure—that was the best she could hope for throughout the rest of this evening. *Was it evening? Or had enough time passed for the early hours of a new day to arrive?*

His hand pressed against her shoulder.

Only years of conditioning kept her from flinching against that touch. With a deep breath and the resignation that came with the knowledge of what would come, Elsbeth forced her body to relax. Tension would only make the pain worse.

His fingertips brushed against the curve of her shoulder and swept down her back. He traced the line of her spine until he came to where her waist narrowed, and then his fingers walked toward her belly. When he pulled her against him, his spicy musk, fetid and rank after a long evening, seeped through the thin cloth of the hood.

Elsbeth made certain not to react. She let him explore, her mind focused on thoughts of brighter days to come. The summer sky would soon brighten with the sun, and the deep blue would pull her to a distant place. With great struggle, her mind detached from her body until she became little more than a spectator in that dark basement.

Master John removed the hood. Hair matted against her tear-streaked face, it was in her mouth, shoved up her nose, and stuck to her eyelashes. With great tenderness, he gathered all the strands, pulling them back over her shoulders to drape between her shoulder blades. The gentleness of his kisses feathered a trail down her skin, eliciting…nothing. No fear. No revulsion. Nothing.

She'd accepted her fate.

Elsbeth breathed out. This was her future; of that, she was certain.

Unless she did something to change it. *But what could a seventeen-year-old girl do?*

He lifted her bound wrists off the hook overhead. The heavy weight of her arms pulled at her sockets. Numb for a moment, she barely registered the ache. The press of his lips settled in the hollow of her throat, soft, gentle, insistent.

And she felt detached from her surroundings, but his words tumbled through her mind.

"You may beg for forgiveness later."

He'd never set a punishment.

What would it hurt to try? It wouldn't. That was the answer. And it had been years since Elsbeth cared about pride.

"Master John," she whispered. "Please," she whimpered. "I'm sorry. I'll be good. Forgive me."

The roving of his hands stilled. His lips lifted from her neck.

She rushed to fill the silence. "I shouldn't have disobeyed. I…please, I beg for your forgiveness although I don't deserve it."

His lips nibbled at her ear, and then he cupped her jaw, twisting her neck to the side. The darkness of his eyes drilled into her.

Deferring to his station, she dropped her gaze. "I'm sorry." And then her body did tremble.

He lifted her in his arms. "My dearest pet, I will always forgive you. All I ever ask is for you to obey." With his promise spoken, he carried her through the room.

Taking another chance, she wrapped her leaden arms around his neck—partly to keep from falling but really more to prove her capitulation. Her survival depended on convincing him that she'd accepted his dominance even if it wasn't true.

As he carried her to the stairs, the bruised and battered form of Forest on the floor had her hitching her breath, and her heart stopped beating. Still and lifeless, he looked so very gentle, small, and fragile. She stared, daring Master John's wrath, until the gentle rise and fall of Forest's chest proved he still lived.

Master John planned to steal her future, but what he and Clark Preston had planned for Forest was worse. She feared for Forest's life. *A year?* That was how long Master John had given her little Beanpole. That couldn't happen.

With her arms wrapped around Master John's neck, she burrowed into his embrace, inhaling his sickly sweet stench. Carried in the arms of her tormentor, Elsbeth was taken to his guest bedroom on the second floor. Master John tucked her into his bed, and she spent the rest of the night in the arms of a madman who'd claimed her as his own.

Ashes to New

CHAPTER TEN

DAWN BROKE WITH a violent fury, the air seething with gusts and driving rain. Thunderstorms had rolled in from the west, bringing enough power to rattle the windows and shake the foundation of the house.

Elsbeth woke, clutching fine linen sheets to her naked form. *Where the hell was she?* Her pulse raced while the fog of her mind struggled to catch up.

It didn't take long for the memories to return. *Where was Master John?* The side of the bed he'd slept in held only rumpled sheets.

Ah, there, on the pillow, was a note. She reached for it, dreading what she would find but feeling relieved to have awoken alone.

My darling,

The day is yours, as work has called me in. I won't be back until late tonight, but I eagerly await your sweet embrace.

The man was twisted in the head, and his words had her stomach roiling. Yanking the sheet off her body, she leaped from the bed. Lightning flashed outside the windows, followed by a rolling long peal of thunder.

Forest!

Had they left him downstairs?

She raced through the upper floor, not caring to explore the one level in the house she'd never ventured in before. Always, she'd believed her time with Clark Preston would end, and she would be free. But she'd been horribly wrong. That realization flooded her with an unsavory wave of emotions.

All this time, she'd thought she was merely passing the time until her eighteenth birthday arrived to free her from the confines of the foster care system. Little had she known how much of a prisoner she was. Master John had said she'd been his from the moment she arrived.

When had this deal been struck?

Her bare feet slapped against the tiles, and her tread was muffled by the long line of Persian rugs in the hall. Her fingers fluttered as she twisted the knob to Forest's bedroom. Inside, the stillness in the air forced her pulse to jump. It hammered in her neck as she confirmed he wasn't in his bed.

She ran to the basement door. Her hands shaking, she slid the lock free of the latch on the door.

Still lying in the same spot on the floor, Forest had curled into a fetal ball. He whimpered. As she approached, his body convulsed.

"It's only me," she whispered.

Forest stilled, but when she touched his shoulder, he flinched.

"Don't," he cried out. "Please, don't touch me."

His aversion to her touch was bothersome. All she wanted was to pull him into a hug and hold him, promising him everything would be okay. *But would it?*

Time ticked by, the seconds devouring the silence, while she sat beside her best friend. Really, Forest meant more to her than that. He was the brother she'd lost. Bound by ties thicker than blood, they'd survived a crucible of anguish. She loved him so hard that her heart broke.

"This is our fate," he said. "We're never leaving this place."

Oh, they were leaving. After five years, she and her Beanpole were going to leave this place and be ripped away from each other. Unless she did something to stop it.

"I hate this." He shifted away. "I hate them."

She reached out to stroke his hair, but pulled back, unsure of how he'd react. "I know. I hate it, too."

"I never thought this would be our path, but I can't see a way to be free of it."

It was a living agony neither of them would ever be free from.

"We've walked through hell." He huffed a laugh, a pathetic and weak noise. "I always thought we'd find a way past it, but we've only traveled deeper. Why us?"

"I don't know." And she didn't.

She didn't know why fate had stolen her parents. She didn't know why they'd taken her baby brother. She hated how she wished he'd died. Without the threat of her baby brother's life, she would have escaped years ago. She hated not knowing if her brother was alive. She despised the knowledge that granted men, such as Clark Preston such power over her life.

"Don't we have a choice?" Defeat hung heavy in his tone. "I just want it all to stop. It hurts so much."

"You'll heal."

They'd both heal.

"I heard what Snowden said." Forest heaved a deep sigh. "I'm going to be lost without you."

As she would be without him.

How was she to respond?

He'd always been her light when darkness shrouded her mind. To see him utterly broken rocked the foundation of her world as much or more than the storm outside tested the integrity of the house.

"Then, we need to change our future," she said, not knowing what that would mean. But she did. A brewing anger had settled in her gut, and it had been growing blacker with each passing moment.

"How?"

There was only one way, and Forest's gentle mind would break with the knowledge.

"I can't fight them." His sobs turned uncontrollable. His entire body shook with his misery. "I'm broken," he said.

"You'll get better. You're the strongest person I know." *And the weakest.*

They'd endured too much. The damage had been done.

Beautifully broken. Emotionally ruined. That defined their existence.

She needed to save him before he was lost forever.

Together, somehow, they would come out of this stronger than they were now. To do that, required an unthinkable plan.

"Come," she said, ignoring his protests when she gripped his shoulders.

Supporting much of his weight, she helped him to his room, and while she thought he'd be more comfortable soaking in her tub, Forest insisted on taking a shower alone. Unwilling to fight the issue even though she was right, Elsbeth helped him to his bathroom. She stood outside, but he managed well enough by himself. He wouldn't let her close when he exited and ambled to his bed. And then, with a face full of fatigue and defeat, he collapsed on his bed.

She left him, her mind in turmoil, and went to prepare for what needed to be done.

CHAPTER ELEVEN

LIKE FOREST, ELSBETH opted for a shower, letting the steam build until it fogged the mirror. A thick layer of suds did the trick, washing the filth down the drain. Wrapping the long length of her hair in a towel, she dressed in a pair of jeans and a white cotton blouse.

She left her room and tiptoed to Forest's bedroom. A quick peek confirmed Forest slumbered although his sleep appeared to be anything but peaceful.

Ideas percolated in her head, and none of them were good. A decision had to be made, however, and she struggled with the implications. As she was faced with a future of slavery for her and the brutality Forest would face in a fighting ring, peace settled quickly beneath her determination.

Now, all that was left to do was to wait out the interminable passage of time.

Elsbeth grabbed her copy of *Wuthering Heights* and curled up on the couch in the great room. For a time, she became someone else and traveled a different path.

Forest woke later in the afternoon, emerging from his room to search the kitchen for something to eat. He said nothing, his vacant stare fortifying her resolve.

Her cell phone buzzed with a text a few minutes prior to five p.m. It was time. Clark Preston would be home. Master John wasn't expected for several hours, giving her a window of opportunity.

Her mind stilled in those few moments while she waited for Clark Preston to arrive. Acceptance brought a ray of hope, something she latched on to because she feared the next few hours. The Porsche rumbled outside, followed by the screeching of the garage door sliding on its rails.

Elsbeth knelt on her rug and counted the eleven steps it took for him to cross the floor.

She completed the greeting ritual, kissing the top of his shoe, lingering for a moment to rest her cheek against the polished leather. His sharp intake of breath made her smile. She'd surprised him.

"Did you miss me, little one?" His voice softened with praise for her uncharacteristic display.

"Yes, sir." She could have said more, but she didn't want to raise his suspicions.

He took the two steps to where Forest stood, his feet spread wide on a base much more solid than his state of mind. She'd tried to get him to talk to her throughout the day, but her Beanpole had remained distant and vacant.

"I have something special planned for you tonight." Clark Preston strode down the hall. "Come."

The order was no different than the thousands that had come before, yet this one felt needful and raw.

Elsbeth rose, and with a glance at Forest, she followed Clark Preston down the hall and to the great room.

Her position was at the edge of the carpet, Forest's place was at the center of the room, and Clark Preston took a seat on the couch. She broke protocol and dared to approach. With her hands clasped before her and head bowed, she walked to stand before him. His eyes widened, surprise muted by the fever of lust brewing behind his stare. Capitalizing on his lust, she lowered to her knees, pressing her cheek against his thigh.

It took less than a breath before his fingers slipped through her hair. He'd always been fascinated by her long hair.

"Little one?"

Lifting her head, she met the fierceness of his eyes and rose to straddle his lap. "Please, sir."

Her gentle gyrations fed his hunger, and his need stiffened behind the zipper of his trousers.

His deep voice broke upon a soft laugh. "You're going to miss me, aren't you?"

Her answer was to snuggle into his eager embrace. She wrapped her arms around him, slipping her fingers between the cushions to grab the hilt of the knife she'd planted between the seam of the cushions. The sound of Forest shifting gave her pause. She'd wanted to spare him this memory, but she had little choice.

Pressing her lips against Clark Preston's throat, she nibbled and sucked while his dick hardened beneath the training he'd instilled in her hips from the tender age of twelve.

With the trail of her kisses angling down his jaw, her grip tightened, as did her resolve. She kissed him then, exciting the man who'd stolen her innocence. He grabbed her breasts, pinching and twisting her nipples. She kissed him deeply, opening her mouth to allow him to take her as he pleased, and while his tongue speared her mouth, she dragged the sharpened blade against his throat.

His startled shout was swallowed by a flood of blood. She lifted off his lap and watched him gurgle on his last breath, feeling nothing but relief.

"Elsbeth?"

Forest's low tone demanded her attention, but she didn't want to miss this moment. It was done. Years of abuse had been silenced with a single cut of flesh.

"Elsbeth?" More insistent now, Forest wouldn't be denied much longer.

Clark Preston's body crumpled. The blood congealed into a thick, sticky mess, dripping down his chest to pool in his lap. Turning her attention to the mess, she stared at her knees.

Anticlimactic. That was the word that came to mind.

He should have suffered more. His death had been far too swift and far too peaceful.

"Elsbeth?" Forest's whisper came from behind.

She dropped the knife and crawled off the couch. His blood coated her inner thighs, and the coppery stench had her gagging.

But they weren't safe yet.

"Call the cops, Bean." Her voice came out monotone, holding much firmer than she'd expected. "They need to get here before Master John returns."

And, from his note, they would have a couple of hours at best, if that long.

"The cops?"

"Yes, call the damn cops." She turned to face him. "They need to get here before John Snowden."

Comprehension dawned in Forest's eyes. He gulped and then looked at the body. "Why?"

Did she tell him what the men had planned for him? She should, and she would, but for now, she needed to get Clark Preston's blood off her body.

CHAPTER TWELVE

THE POLICE FOUND Elsbeth tucked in a corner of her shower. Water poured down. Steam filled the room. Blood still coated her legs. She'd had every intention of washing away Clark Preston's residue, but her hands had been shaking too hard. Then, the tears had come. She had no real idea how long she'd been waiting. She didn't really care.

But she was waiting. There was only one outcome that could follow murder. She'd do it again in a heartbeat and without regret.

All that mattered was Forest and the continued safety of her baby brother. They'd wanted to destroy Forest, pitting him in whatever fighting ring they'd mentioned. John Snowden was right. Forest wouldn't have lasted a year. His gentle nature would have hastened his death.

He wasn't the only one she worried about. Her brother's safety had hinged on the obedience she gave to Clark Preston. He'd held the constant threat of harm over her head if she dared to disobey. Where her brother had wound up, she didn't know, but Clark Preston had. That fear had ruled her life even if she kept it tucked far away. She didn't even remember what he looked like. He was an infant when the accident had happened. Now she would never know.

Infants were much easier to adopt than traumatized girls. She hadn't seen him since the accident, but she had been told he'd gone to a good home. When she thought of him, her imagination would bring forth the image of what he must look like with the passing years. He was always surrounded by faceless parents, who loved and adored him.

Her future remained uncertain, but time continued its relentless march. The cops arrived.

The cops brought in a female to talk her out of the shower. Elsbeth's mind was numb. She moved on autopilot, lathering with soap, rinsing, washing her hair, and then drying everything off. The lady cop walked with her into the closet and picked out a shirt while Elsbeth tugged on a pair of jeans and toed on her shoes. The cotton blouse slid over her head and settled around her waist.

Now what? She turned to the cop. "Are you going to arrest me?"

John Snowden had planned to steal her future by turning her into his slave. Now, she'd handed over her freedom to the justice system—and willingly, too. She'd rather spend the rest of her life in jail than spend another moment under the power of men like Clark Preston and John Snowden.

The woman put her hand on Elsbeth's shoulder. "We need to ask a few questions."

"Forest didn't—"

"Shh." The woman had warm brown eyes and black hair tied into a bun. The corners of her eyes dipped down, mirroring the sadness etched on her face. "Is there anything you need? A purse maybe?"

The badge pinned to the woman's chest identified her last name as Naples, but Elsbeth didn't know how to address the cop. She didn't think the woman was a detective, based upon nothing more than the woman's age. *Weren't detectives older?*

Thoughts moved like molasses in her head, and a kind of buzzing filled her ears. *Must be the early stages of shock.*

A purse? She had one but where? And why? Wouldn't the cops simply take everything and put it in one of those plastic bag things?

Elsbeth moved to her room, shadowed closely by Officer Naples. Her purse hung from the chair by her desk, but there wasn't anything important in it, except for her school ID. She had no driver's license and no money. Clark Preston might have allowed her and Forest to attend school—because the foster system frowned upon homeschooling of foster children—but he had drawn the line at the independence or freedom a driver's license would have granted.

Elsbeth picked up her purse and turned to the cop, seeking direction.

A gentle gaze greeted Elsbeth.

"Come." The woman gestured. "Detective Grady wants to question you."

The cavernous house had always been a place of echoes, but now, the walls practically buzzed with activity. Dozens of cops filled the kitchen, the great room, and even trickled down the long hall leading to the front of the house. They worked with quick efficiency, collecting evidence.

Elsbeth scanned the sea of blue, seeking Forest. A group of men were clustered around the couch. One shot pictures of the crime scene while others stood, pointing, conversing, and taking notes. All that evidence would seal her fate.

Officer Naples took her arm and steered her toward the front of the house. Elsbeth was guided to the formal dining room where the woman pulled out a chair and told her to have a seat. It was an order, not a request. *Easy enough.* Elsbeth had been taking orders for years.

Across the way, Forest's shock of blond hair was unmistakable against the men in their dark uniforms. He was taller than most of them. Her little Beanpole was growing up, but he was still skinny as a rail. It made him look smaller, more fragile, than he really was.

What were they doing in the study?

Forest was speaking with the men, his arms animated and his fingers pointing all around the room. A pair of cops stood behind Clark Preston's desk, the glow of the monitor lighting their faces in a pale light. They had another photographer in that room. Why the man was snapping photos in there was beyond her. A couple of others were combing through files.

Forest's head lifted over the men. His gaze caught hers, and he dared a smile.

A smile.

His gentle nature remained. He lifted his hand but not to wave. The gesture was meant more as an acknowledgment.

Forest took a step toward her, but the man he was talking to pressed a hand against Forest's chest. A scowl formed on Forest's face, and then resignation filled his eyes. She understood. The cops would be keeping them separate until they could ask their questions.

She took in a deep breath and prepared for her interrogation.

A thickset man wandered down the hall. He stepped into the dining room and paused to take in her shaking form. Elsbeth tilted her head to meet his expression. Bushy thick hair framed the stern lines of his face. Despite his fearsome appearance, she relaxed, thankful he wasn't one of the many men Clark Preston had brought into the house.

"Your brother says your name is Elsbeth?" His soft tone blanketed her with reassurance. She knew, instinctually that she could trust him. "May I call you Elsbeth, or is there another name you prefer?"

Biting her lower lip, she shook her head. "Elsbeth is fine."

"It's a pretty name." He pulled back a chair and took out a pad of paper from the breast pocket of his blazer. "Elsbeth, my name is Detective Grady. I need to ask you a few questions. Do you think you can answer them?"

She nodded.

He explained her rights, but she had nothing to hide.

"I killed him."

Detective Grady nodded. "Yes, that's what your brother said over the phone."

"My foster brother," she corrected. "We're not related."

He made a note on his pad of paper. "He explained, but I'd like to hear from you what happened and why, if that's possible."

It was more than possible.

Elsbeth told Detective Grady everything. Officer Naples' expression paled when Elsbeth detailed some of the sexual abuse. Eventually, she excused herself, but she returned a few minutes later with two glasses of water. Elsbeth took one and continued.

When social services arrived an hour later, she breathed another sigh of relief, grateful for yet another unfamiliar face.

She told the cops what John Snowden had said about paying off her caseworker. She even mentioned the judge. They asked her for names and a description of John Snowden.

Activity picked up in the library. The men brought in empty boxes. More men joined them. There were very few women. And, as she talked, those men packed the boxes with the contents of Clark Preston's library.

Another group arrived a bit later. They swept in and out, removing the body, and still, she told her story. Detective Grady shifted in his seat during some of the more graphic descriptions, but his pen scratched over the pad, his writing furious to keep pace.

The woman from social services left to speak with Forest and then came back a few minutes later. "Detective," she said, "it's getting late, and the kids need to eat. How much longer will this take?"

He tapped his notebook with the tip of his pen. "I think we're nearly done." His gaze felt solid, trustworthy, and nestled into her heart. "Do you like pizza?"

"Am I going to jail?"

He glanced at the social worker and then shook his head. "No, I don't think so."

Those words broke the dam holding back her emotions. Elsbeth cracked, and tears poured down her cheeks. She wrapped her arms around herself and rocked as the world disappeared.

It was over. It was all finally over.

But, as much as her belly ached for food, she wanted only one thing. She needed Forest's hug. She wanted him to say everything would be all right, but he wouldn't touch her.

Elsbeth cried her agony until she found herself pulled into the embrace of a stranger.

CHAPTER THIRTEEN

IT HAD BEEN months since Elsbeth had taken Clark Preston's life.

As she dressed for her trial, her mind was blank and empty. Judge Johnson, their old caseworker, and a few others they had named, had been arrested that night. John Snowden had never been found, escaping, no doubt, overseas to avoid extradition.

The night she'd killed Clark Preston, Detective Grady had bought pizza, and she and Forest had eaten their last meal in the dining room of that wretched house.

She never got that hug. Forest still wouldn't touch her. He couldn't touch her, but he never left her side. Always, Forest was there, supporting her through the darkest times, except when she needed a shoulder to cry on.

"You almost ready?" Forest walked into her room without knocking. He picked up her bag and swung it over his shoulder.

She adjusted her skirt and pulled at the pink blouse. "How do I look?"

"Like you can take on the world."

Maybe she could. A sense of becoming something new loomed on the horizon. There was only this one thing to do before she could contemplate her future.

"I don't know about the world," she said, "but I'm ready to put this behind me. I hate this. I hate this happened to us...to you."

"It's the path fate chose for us, Elz," he said. "We have to walk it."

"But it's hell."

With the investigation, the questioning, and the series of pretrials that had followed, Elsbeth had pulled out of school. She had taken her GED and sent applications to several pre-med programs. Forest had failed the GED twice before accepting he'd have to go back and complete his senior year. He hadn't wanted to go without her, but she'd convinced him it was the right thing to do. That meant he had to leave her alone with her thoughts every day, his fingers fluttering over hers in an awkward good-bye.

Forest had finally revealed the reason behind his aversion to her touch. The conditioning instilled by John Snowden made him react in ways he wasn't ready to process. She lost Forest's hugs because of what John Snowden had done.

Self-defense.

That was the trial strategy. After the cops discovered videos buried in Clark Preston's things, confirming the story she and Forest had told, there was little doubt as to the abuse she and Forest had suffered. However, there were procedures. She'd been appointed an attorney. Her case, he'd explained, would be dismissed.

She never told anyone how she'd planned Clark Preston's death. Well, she'd told Forest, but he wasn't just anyone. *Premeditation* was a word she understood—as well as the consequences associated with it. They'd made a vow to take that secret to the grave together. There were some questions about the knife. The how had been hidden by the fog of her descriptions. She'd been out of her mind, Forest had claimed, and in many ways, that wasn't far from the truth.

Today's trial would determine her guilt or innocence—or at least the official version.

Forest opened the door and led her outside to the crispness of the spring morning.

She stopped and inhaled. "It smells so new."

He smiled. "It does, doesn't it?"

"Yeah. A new beginning, I suppose." She spun in a circle, soaking in the sun. "I feel like we've walked through hell together and survived."

"Something like that."

"Is there hope for us?" *Would the scars ever heal?*

Forest pointed at the sky. "Do you see that?"

The heat of the sun warmed her face. "The sun?"

He shook his head. "No, the sky. Do you see the sky?"

"What about it?"

"It reminds me of you. Not this sky, but the summer sky. It's a deeper blue, I think."

"I don't understand."

"When I was in the basement, I would spend hours looking out that tiny window."

"Forest…"

She hated the swell of memories brewing in his gaze. He had the palest blue eyes, and they shimmered now with a glaze of tears, turning them nearly silver.

"Let me finish." He took in a deep breath and then continued, "There was always that small patch of the outside world. When things were at their worst, I would stare out the window and think of you."

"Me?"

"Yeah," he said with a half-laugh. "You kept me sane."

"How?"

The summer had been hardest on him. She'd been forced to serve, but Forest had survived torture.

"They ruined me, but through it all, I kept thinking, *Elsbeth is so strong.* Your belief that things would get better was as endless as the summer sky. I wanted to be like you."

"Oh, Forest, I'm not like that. I'm emotionally ruined."

"You're beautifully broken, and you were my summer sky, my light in the darkness." He reached into his pocket and pulled out an envelope. "I was going to wait to give this to you, but I wanted you to see it before court. I want you to have something to look forward to." The corner of his lip pulled up into a smirk. "I might have peeked." He shoved the envelope into her hand.

An official seal on the front had her heart beating. "It's a thin letter."

Thin letters were bad. Rejections came with thin letters.

"Open it." A grin filled his face.

With shaking hands, Elsbeth ripped the paper and read the first line. "Oh my God!" She fell to her knees and sobbed.

He knelt beside her. "I'm going to build you a hospital, Elz. I'm going to build you the biggest and best hospital in the world. This"—he jabbed the paper—"is your future."

"Oh, Forest, you can't build me a hospital, but I really appreciate the thought."

His face cracked a smile. "Don't tell me what I can't do. We'll start with your tuition, and I'll make the rest."

Whatever. She didn't care. She'd been accepted into one of the prestigious six-year programs. She was going to be a doctor. Her dream was becoming a reality.

******

Self-defense.

That was what the official documents stated, and because she was a minor, the records would be sealed. None of this would follow her into her new life.

Forest's future would start tomorrow. He'd officially turn eighteen and be free of social services. He'd already put a deposit down on an apartment, and he had his bags packed. Nothing could hurt them now.

Forest might be averse to her touch, but she didn't care.

Elsbeth hugged him tight. "It's over, Bean! It's finally over."

She'd taken to calling him Bean more often than not, and he didn't seem to mind. The nickname suited him.

Her lawyer pulled her aside after the hearing. "Congratulations," he said. "I have something for you."

"You do?" Her heart had never felt so full.

Elsbeth had no idea how she would meet her goals, but she knew two things. She wasn't going to jail, and in a few short months, after she figured out finances, she would begin an entirely new path.

The grin on Forest's face had her suspicious. Whatever was happening, he was in on it.

Her lawyer pulled out a stack of papers. "Well, your brother came to me with an idea."

"Bean, what did you do?"

He grabbed the papers from her lawyer and held them to his chest. "Well, I thought you needed a way to wash away the past. And seeing how you're going to be a doctor..." He gave her the papers.

She read the top of the page. "A name change?"

"Yeah." He puffed out his chest. "I was thinking...why not put all of this behind you? Start out fresh. New name, new life, new you."

"But I have no idea what name I would use."

He took the papers and turned to the second page. "I was thinking Skye Summers."

An odd-sounding name. "Why..."

But then his words about the basement came back. The summer sky that had gotten him through the toughest times. Her hope, as limitless as the summer sky, had brought him peace. *His summer sky.*

"Oh, I love it."

Forest kissed the bridge of her nose. "My summer Skye." He leaned back, his touch too fleeting. "It suits you."

It did, and she loved what it meant—to him and to her. "And you're my little Beanpole."

He coughed into his fist. "Maybe not so little anymore, but I was thinking of changing mine."

"How about Bean?"

"I like Forest," he said. "Forest Summers."

The expectant look on his face had her heart leaping.

"Like brother and sister?"

He nodded. "But you can call me Bean." His gesture encompassed the sky. "It's not a summer sky, but it's nearly as blue."

Her lawyer cleared his throat. "It's a bit of paperwork, but we can get it done"

She turned to Forest. "You planned this, didn't you?"

He curled his lower lip inward. "A birthday gift for my sister." His expression turned troubled, and a flicker of doubt flashed in his eyes. "We'll always have that, my summer Skye. Won't we? We'll always have each other?"

"Always, Bean. We'll always have each other." And she believed every word.

<<<< THE END >>>>

Final Thoughts

I hope you enjoyed this book as much as I enjoyed writing it. If you did, then please consider leaving a review. I would love to hear what you think. A sentence is all it takes, but a book lives or dies based upon its reviews. If you enjoyed reading this story, let other people know. Friend recommendations are the strongest catalyst for readers' purchase decisions! And I'd love to be able to continue bringing the characters and stories from My-Mind-to-the-Page.

Second, call or e-mail a friend and tell them about this book. If you really want them to read it, gift it to them. If you prefer digital friends, please use the "Recommend" feature of Goodreads to spread the word.

Third, please "like" the Ellie Masters Dark Romance Facebook page.
https://www.facebook.com/elliemastersdarkromance.

Or visit my blog https://elliemasters.com/, where you can find out more about my writing process and personal life. And come visit The EDGE: Dark Discussions where we'll have a chance to talk about my works, their creation, and maybe what the future has in store for my writing.
https://www.facebook.com/groups/EllieMasters.TheEdge/

Thank you so much for your support!

Love,
Ellie

Ashes to New

Novels by Ellie Masters

Heart's Insanity: an Angel Fire Rock Romance
Publisher: JEM Publishing, LLC
Released August 2016
books2read.com/HeartsInsanity

Blurb: Skye Summers endured a tragic past. She wants what the past stole, and despite lingering scars, she's surviving and thriving. Now she cures the sick, heals the wounded, and takes care of those clinging to life. The only person she can't heal is herself, because Skye is too broken for love.

Ash Dean has it all: Fame, fortune, and the adoration of screaming fans. The constant parties, drugs, alcohol, and an endless string of one-night stands are taking their toll. He gives and his fans take, until he's lost within the crowd. He wants someone to see him for the man he wishes to be rather than the one he's become.

One fate…

Two lives…

Three Days…

No sex.

That's the proposition…

It would be insane to accept and Skye's a fool to agree, but she's tired of playing it safe.

It's time to take a leap of faith, besides what could go wrong?

Ellie Masters

* * * * * *

CHANGING ROLES
Publisher: Loose Id
Released March 2016
books2read.com/ChangingRoles

Blurb: Kate Summers's career on the Police Force came to an implosive end when the Mayor's wife exposed her secret life as the Mistress of Pain. Kate lost not only her detective's badge, but something much more valuable. She lost her confidence as a Mistress of men.

She now scrapes by as a private investigator, feeding off the misery of others. When the Mayor and his wife ask her to investigate the murder of their daughter, Kate faces a difficult decision. To follow the leads, she must reenter the world that destroyed her career and go undercover as a submissive to a noted Dom. Only Kate swore she'd never endure the submissive role again.

Yet Jake Davenport is the one dominant fearless enough to not only challenge her rules, but break them. While accepting her new role and the erotic thrill it brings her is difficult enough, Jake's complicated past raises many questions. As her investigation progresses, the man she's fallen in love with might just be her number one suspect.

About Ellie Masters

Ellie Masters has been exploring the worlds of romance, dark erotica, science fiction, and fantasy, by reading and writing the stories she wants to read. When not writing, Ellie can be found outside, where her passion for all things outdoor reigns supreme: off-roading, riding ATVs, scuba diving, hiking, and breathing fresh air are top on her list.

With the release of her debut novel, Ellie is pleased to add "author" to her life's list of accomplishments. Wife, lover, and mother are her most treasured roles, but Ellie has played many parts: counter girl at a McDonalds, a research assistant in a Nanofabrication facility, a rocket scientist who designed ICBM guidance systems, and a physician—which only proves that anything in life is possible if you set goals and never give up.

She has lived all over the United States—east, west, north, south and central—but grew up under the Hawaiian sun. She's also been privileged to have lived overseas, experiencing other cultures and making lifelong friends. Now, Ellie is proud to call herself a Southern transplant, learning to say y'all and "bless her heart" with the best of them. She lives with her beloved husband, two children who refuse to flee the nest, and four fur-babies; three cats who rule the household, and a dog who wants nothing other than for the cats to be his best friends. The cats have a different opinion regarding this matter.

Ellie's favorite way to spend an evening is curled up on a couch, laptop in place, watching a fire, drinking a good wine, and bringing forth all the characters from her mind to the page and hopefully into the hearts of her readers.

Made in the USA
Middletown, DE
06 August 2024

58602402R00051